"It is the knowledge that I will die, that creates the focus that I bring to being alive. The urgency of accomplishment. The need to express love. Now. Not later. If we live forever, why ever even get out of bed in the morning... because you always have tomorrow.
I don't fear death; I fear living a life where I could have accomplished something I didn't. That's what I fear."

— Neil deGrasse Tyson, May 2016

"If life were eternal, wouldn't it lose much of what gives it shape, structure, meaning, and purpose? One of the things that makes things pleasurable, is that they come to an end. Death is a natural part of life. It makes sense for us to try not to be afraid of this, but instead to come to terms with it. Then, we can focus on finding meaning and purpose in the here and now, making the most of the one life we know we have, and helping others to do the same. When we do die, we will live on: in the work we've done, and in the memories of the other people who's lives we have been part of."

— Stephen Fry, *narrating an animation by British Humanist Association*

For FREE BOOK GIVEAWAYS and news, 'like' us at Facebook.com/AnnabelleAndAiden

Copyright © 2018 by Imaginarium Press, LLC. All rights reserved. First Edition.
ISBN 978-0-9978066-6-3
Published in the United States by Imaginarium Press, LLC.
Annabelle & Aiden is a trademark of Imaginarium Press, LLC.

AnnabelleAndAiden.com

Where Were We Before We Were Born?
A Foreword by Michael Shermer

Imagine nothing. Go ahead. What do you see? I picture dark empty space devoid of galaxies, stars, planets, people, and even light. But not only would there be no matter or energy, there would be no space or time either. Not even darkness. And there would be no sentient conscious life to observe the nothingness. Just... nothing. No. Thing. Picture that. You can't.

This is what comes to mind when I imagine where I was before I was born. Try it. Imagine where you were before you were born. You can't because you didn't exist before you were born.

The same problem arises when we ask ourselves what happens when we die. Go ahead and try to conjure up that image. What comes to mind? Do you see your body as part of a scene, perchance presented in a casket surrounded by family and friends at your funeral? Or maybe you see yourself in a hospital bed after expiring from an illness, or on the floor of your home following a fatal heart attack? None of these scenarios—or any others your imagination might conjure—are possible, because in all cases in order to observe or imagine a scene you must be alive and conscious. If you are dead you are neither. You can no more visualize yourself after you die than you can imagine no universe or picture yourself before you were born.

Thus it is we really have nothing to fear about death because we cannot experience it. By definition, to experience anything you must be alive, and death is the cessation of life. So... quit thinking about it and get back to living your life in a way that matters!

What does it mean to live a life that matters? What is a meaningful and purposeful life, anyway? I have given a lot of thought to this question, and I have written an entire book trying to answer it. Along the way I read all of the great scholars, philosophers, theologians, and scientists who have addressed the ultimate question of life, death, and meaning, but in the end I must confess that the most deeply moving account I have ever come across is the one you are holding in your hands. In only 200 words this beautiful story captures what 2000 years of wisdom writing could not. Read it. Then read it again. And then get back to living your life in a way that matters because now you know how.

—Michael Shermer is the Publisher of *Skeptic* magazine, a monthly columnist for *Scientific American*, and a Presidential Fellow at Chapman University. He is the New York Times Bestselling author of *The Believing Brain, The Moral Arc,* and *Heavens on Earth: The Scientific Search for the Afterlife, Immortality,* and *Utopia*

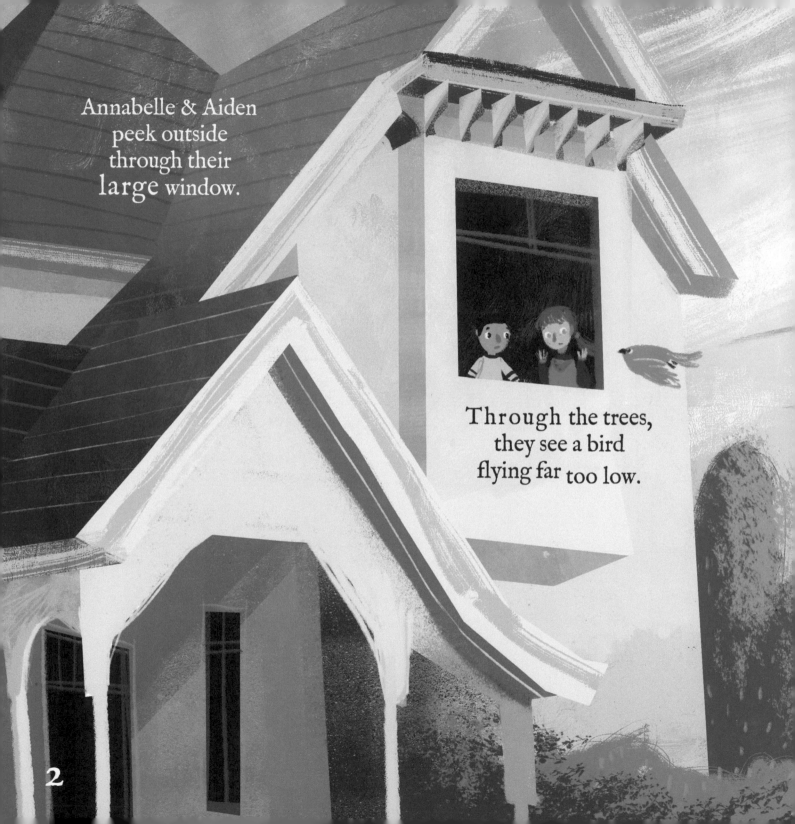

Annabelle & Aiden
peek outside
through their
large window.

Through the trees,
they see a bird
flying far too low.

2

The wind blows hard behind its wings.
It's going way too fast!

It tries to fly over the house,
but bangs into the glass!

3

They **run** outside to find the bird.
They see its crooked bill.
Its eyes **closed**, its belly up.
Its body silent still.

4

All the friends were gathered
and stood around that bird.
Even Tom was deep in thought,
and not a sound was heard.

Annabelle asked, "What happens
when we have to say goodbye?
What happens when we leave this life?
What happens when we die?"

6

Aiden said, **"**This makes me *scared.*
I may need to pretend,
that even though our brains turn off,
that this is not the end.

7

"Maybe there's a magic part of us that floats above, that sees, hears and feels the **things** that dreamers can speak of.

Many have reported NDEs (or "near-death experiences"): a feeling of being detached from the body, levitation, security, or reliving old memories, which some use as evidence for an afterlife.

8

"Maybe to a place filled with chocolate kangaroos. And cookie hats, and flying fish, and pink marshmallow shoes.

Hypotheses and theories abound, from hallucination, false-memories, spikes in brain activity, or wish-fulfillment, as the brain's state is altered by oxygen deprivation. Studies are ongoing.

"And bullies go to a place where beds are full of ants. Where toenail soup is all they eat, in prickly underpants!"

Skeptisaurus says, "Maybe. But is there **evidence**? Anything's **possible**, but do you think it makes sense?

"We don't yet have much reason to think any of that's true. (At least not nearly as much as for why we would want to.)

But *before* you cry or whine,
complain, moan or bawl,
learn the things we **do** know:
the greatest things of all!

"You'll see
the truth is just as great;
you don't have to pretend!
You're right about one thing,
my boy,
that death is not the end...

While your brain and your body
may have had their l a s t act,
their energy never dies;
that's a scientific fact!

Your atoms will spread out
to rejoin the universe,
as flowers or rain showers,
or as stardust they'll d i s p e r s e.

The Laws Of Thermodynamics
1. Energy cannot be created nor
destroyed. It can only change,
or flow through space.
2. The entropy of any isolated
system always increases.
3. The entropy of a system
approaches a constant value
as the temperature approaches
absolute zero.

Every piece of you stays
right here; that doesn't change.
The only difference might be
you're just differently arranged.

13

Every single vibration
that you've ever made,
every particle or atom
that bounced off your face,

or was swayed by your smile
or the touch of your hair,
will be forever changed by you.
That will always be there.

With the memories you leave
for the people that you love,
whom you have changed forever,
in more ways than you dream of."

14

Fingernails: 6 mos

Muscles 15 yrs

How long it takes for body parts to be replaced in their entirety

Stomach lining: 2-9 days

Eye lens and much of your heart: never

Hair: 2-7 yrs

"Fine," young Aiden said,
"But our bodies will be changed!"
"True," said Skeptisaurus,
"Yes, quite differently arranged.

"But even now, as you live,
it changes every day.
You get new bones, skin and lips
as the old ones shed away."

16

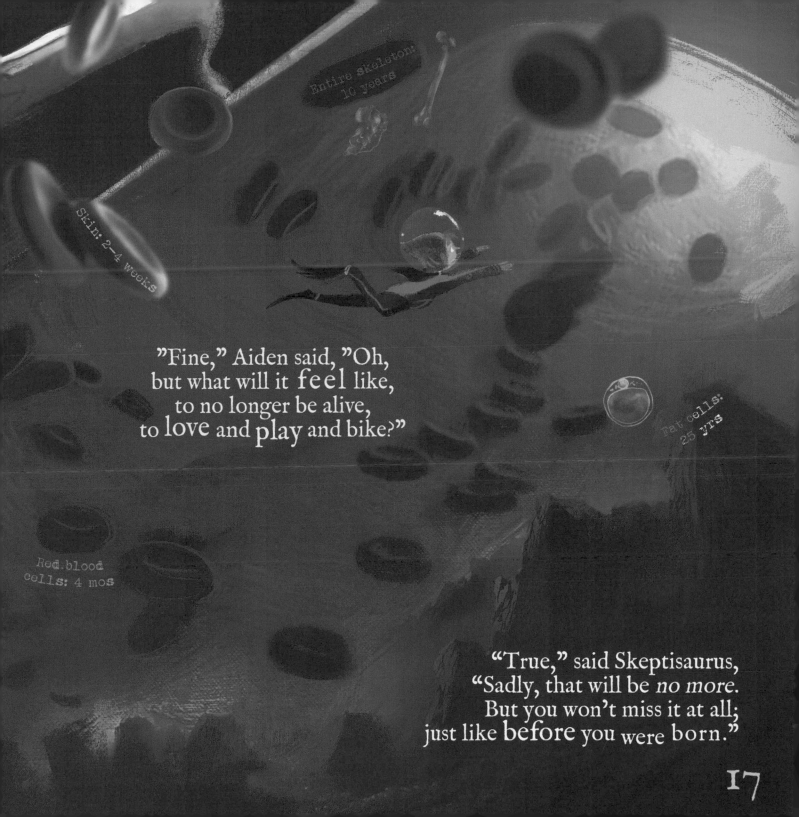

Entire skeleton:
10 years

Skin: 2—4 weeks

"Fine," Aiden said, "Oh,
but what will it feel like,
to no longer be alive,
to love and play and bike?"

Fat cells:
25 yrs

Red blood
cells: 4 mos

"True," said Skeptisaurus,
"Sadly, that will be *no more*.
But you won't miss it at all;
just like before you were born."

17

"Still," Annabelle said,
"How much *better* would it be,
oh, if we could live f o r e v e r ?
All the things that we could see!

18

I'd go to Paris and New York
and eat **every** different food!
Drive a boat around the world,
and fly in a *hot air balloon*.

I'd always stay a little girl.
My friend's hands I'd **always** hold.
I'd spend time with those I love,
and I'd watch as they grow old."

19

"Then what?" said Wise Owl,
"Oh, but then what would you do?
Would it *still* feel **good** to play
more **games** or eat *another* food?

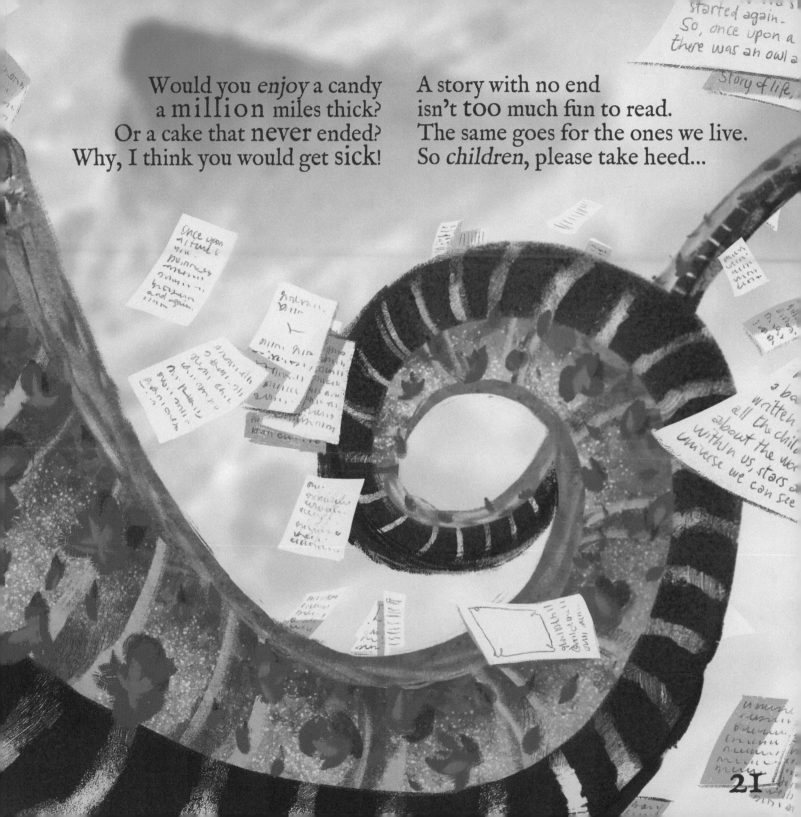

Would you *enjoy* a candy
a m i l l i o n miles thick?
Or a cake that **never** ended?
Why, I think you would get sick!

A story with no end
isn't **too** much fun to read.
The same goes for the ones we live.
So *children*, please take heed...

One thing that makes things special,
is knowing that they end.
That's what makes our lives
so **precious**.
And each moment
with our friends.

So...

eat that cake,
sled that hill,
laugh so hard
it hurts your chest.
And to yourself
and others,
you should be
your very best!

Appreciate small things,
like the sunlight in your hair,
Or wild piggyback rides
and all the things we get to share.

Oh, how lucky that we're here!
We get to give it our best shot!
Like this bird. How he soared!
How he gave it all he got!

Now he'll **change** to something else,
from our fair blue-feathered friend.
But his energy and atoms, well,
their journey never ends."

"Goodbye, bird," Aiden smiled,
"We won't EVER forget you.
But now it's time for us to go.
There's SO much for us to do."

SPECIAL THANKS to Kesley Maurine, Astrid Eugenia Hatfield-Ladd, Abigail & Selah Vinzant Ben Erdin, Jennifer Erdin, Josh Erdin, Elaine Volk & Lillian Volk, Kita, Maddox Sheehan, Chloe Leigh Rebisz, Micah & Olivia Nordlund, Amelia Elidi Nguyen, In memory of the beloved Arlene Wyatt and Our Pal and "Grampa", Robert E. Giancarlo, Kieran MZ Wood, Megan Sinclair, Matthew Weidman, Kristian Amber Kreis, Amanda Gall, Gabriel John Lombardo & Elias Joseph Lombardo, Allison Washington Madelyn Washington, Etta Black, The JETS 134, Laura Curtis, Paul Taggart, Nicola Taggart, Elijah Reader, Sophia Far, Persephone Soleil Taylor / Osiris Lucian Taylor, Ella Lauffer, Cameron Ronald Robert Fitzpatrick, Elliot Coffing, Marulanda Family, Carina Lynn, Christian Wetzel, Glenn Luther, Hadley Wells, Bryan Marten, Innes Family, Remco Bailey, Peyton Hincy, Cambria Hincy, Jacob and Samus, Chrysalis Ashton, Harris Family, Aiden Curtis-Frank Jones, Jude Gosnell Layla Gosnell, Nila and Eli Granillo, Bake Levesque, Clinton Sands, Liam Holzer, Theodosis "Sakis" Efthimiadis, Megan Efthimiadis, Carlos A. "Nasi" Efthimiadis, Rachel H. Pingitore, Griffin Dexter Frick, Susan Carman, The Lane Family, Maximus Rolando Ghirarduzzi, Jonah Winnett, Julie Daellenbach, Dule, Lianne Robinson, Maxwell Lubaski, Alena Sofia Liopiros, Izabella Rosa Young, Eric Isfeld, Ken McKnight, Seamus McEnulty, Shepard McEnulty, Myra Rubinstein, Richard Watkins, Meek & Hertzog kids, Philip Flowers, Victoria, Felcyn Brickner, Kristy Williams, Creatures Drawing Deck, Imogen Hoenig, Cameron Goble, Nathan and Erin Dooley, Jude Franklyn(stein), Lucia Zaldivar, Abby Schwartzlow, Landon Becker, Ackerley Becker, Stephanie Davis, Cynara Stites, Nicole Vykoukal, Bobby, Michael P. Toeniskoetter, Natania Annie Belle Wilson, Dawn Klingensmith, Bethanie Petitpas Queen of Everything, Marshall W Ivey, Caris Allen, The Cunninghame Family, Ashley King, William King, Amy Huber, Jared Scott Krenrick, Baranco-Bushnell, Anita Phagan, Wood Family, Mack Swiney, Amanda Von Der Lohe, Robin Rudd, Abby Taylor, Dave Guin, Lindi Marie Judson, Kieran Trent and Tristan Trent, Team Lawlis, Bonnie Yelverton, Sam & Kate Dyer, Adaline Isla Ross, Marcus Marzolf, Kemper Thomas, The Hansen Family, Tori Rillera, Edward Daniel Hinnebusch, Andrew Matthew Hinnebusch, Bella Meola Burns, The Olivotto Family, Carson Yi Lee, Parker Ren Lee, Cami Roylance, Jaimee, Adele, Ryker, Blanca Sanchez & Karla Escobedo, Julie Hermann Welch, Shlomo Zippel, Neely Reed, Linda Reilly, Zetta J. Snyder, Mel Goeke, Bernadette, Leon Oñate-Enrile, Phinneaus G. Witherington, JPeer, Lil' Boy, Ethan Michael Thompson, Ellie Spivak, Ember Tate, Kingsley Tate, Lars & Louise Hogan, Indio Franqui, Sophia G. Williamson, Julia F. Williamson, DuPuie Family, Coralea Pacha Cobos, Lucia Cobos, Noa Becker, Elijah Becker, Amitai Hepner, Luke & Liza Martin, Conrad C Daly, Jarrett Kenneth York. In memory of Jeffrey Palmer Stone, Thomas Adcock, Amelia Adcock, Ava Adcock, Connie Adcock, and Zoe Wardle.

Thanks a lot,
Windex

CPSIA information can be obtained
at www.ICGtesting.com
Printed in the USA
BVHW010355110223
658208BV00002B/192